WHERE IS MONKEY?

A Beaver Book
Published by Arrow Books Limited
62-5 Chandos Place, London WC2N 4NW
An imprint of Century Hutchinson Ltd

London Melbourne Sydney Auckland
Johannesburg and agencies throughout the world

First published in Great Britain by Hutchinson Children's Books 1987

Beaver edition 1988
Reprinted 1989

© Lemniscaat b.v. Rotterdam 1986

Printed in Italy by Grafiche AZ, Verona

ISBN 0 09 955360 0

WHERE IS MONKEY?

DIETER SCHUBERT

A story without words

BEAVER BOOKS

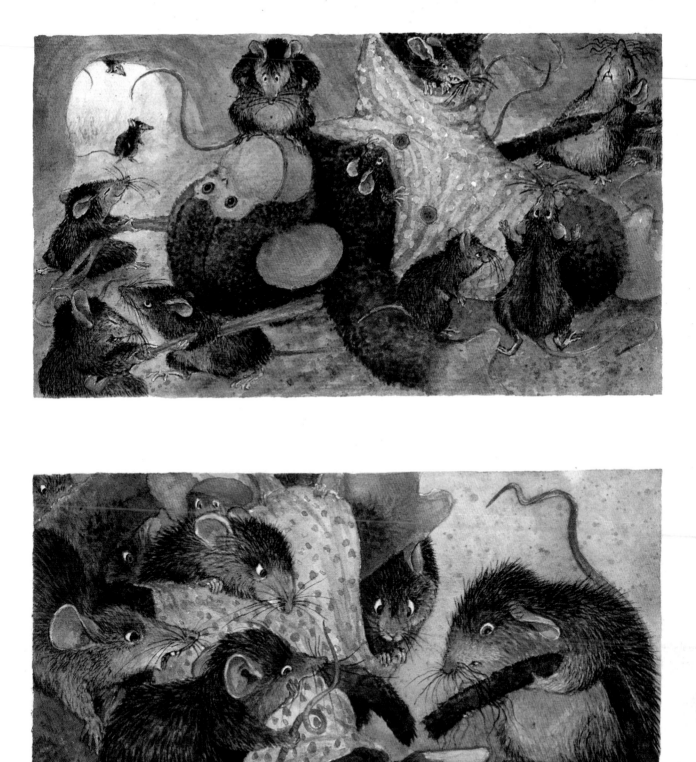

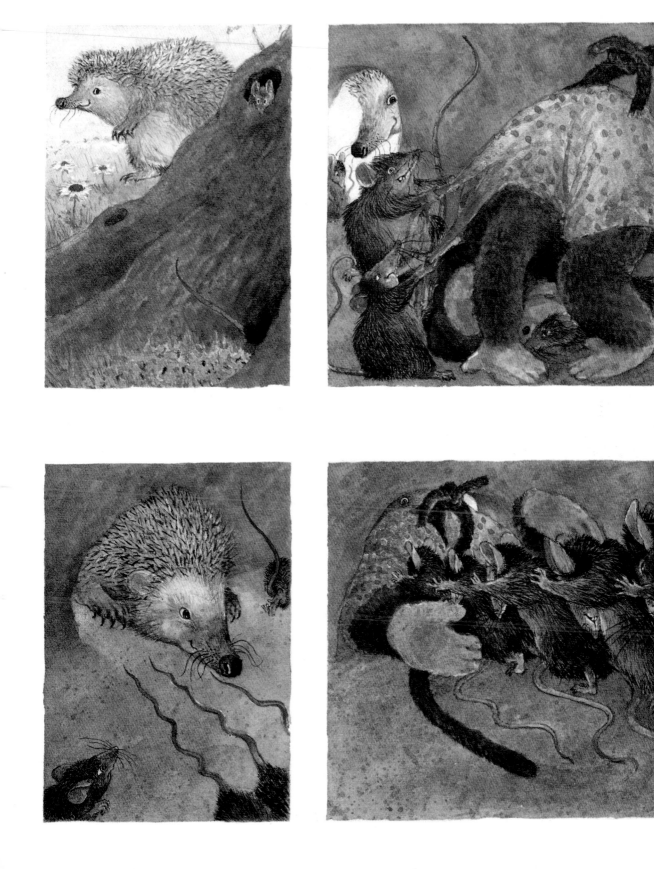

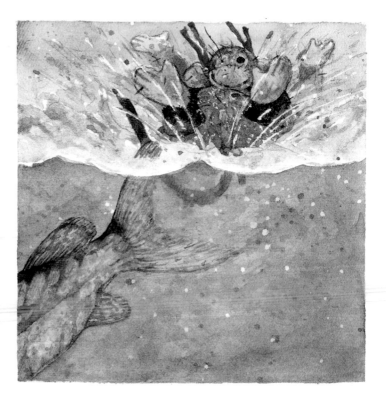

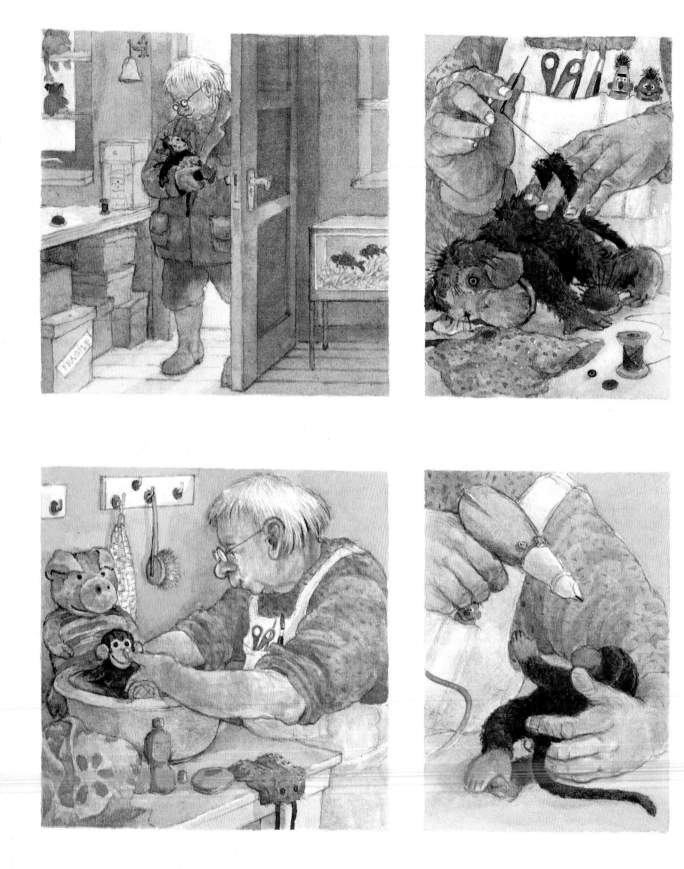

Other titles in the Beaver/Sparrow Picture Book series: